Contents

Chapter One

Jack was watching the Olympics on
the television.

His favourite event was the high jump.

"I wish I could jump that high!"

thought Jack, goggle-eyed.

I AM READING

Jumping Jack

A. H. BENJAMIN

Illustrated by
GARRY PARSONS

For Flynn A.H.B
To Oliver & Edward G.P.

KINGFISHER

First published 2009 by Kingfisher
an imprint of Macmillan Children's Books
a division of Macmillan Publishers Limited
20 New Wharf Road, London N1 9RR
Basingstoke and Oxford
Associated companies throughout the world
www.panmacmillan.com

ISBN: 978-0-7534-1778-2

Text copyright © A. H. Benjamin 2009
Illustrations copyright © Garry Parsons 2009

The moral right of the author and illustrator has been asserted.

2 4 6 8 9 7 5 3 1
1TR/0209/WKT/SC/115MA/C

A CIP catalogue record for this book is available from the British Library.

Printed in China

Just then his uncle walked into the room. He was a sailor. He always brought Jack unusual presents. "Look what I've got for you!" he said, rattling a jar.

"What is it?" frowned Jack.

"Jumping beans!" smiled his uncle.

"They are from South America!"

"Do they really jump?" asked Jack.

"Of course they do," replied his uncle.

To show Jack, he put a few beans on the coffee table.

They started jumping like mad.

Click! Click! Click! They went all over
the place.

One hit the TV screen.

Another struck

the ceiling, bounced

back down and hit

the cat's nose.

Jack laughed with

delight.

He could hardly

believe his eyes.

"Wow, they do jump!" he cried

excitedly. "They're going to be fun!"

And they were . . .

Chapter Two

Then one day Grandma came to stay. She knew nothing about the jumping beans. So when she found them in the kitchen one morning she cooked them for Jack's breakfast.

Jack was in a hurry to go to school
that day. He did not realize what they
were until he had gobbled up the lot!

"But they weren't to eat!" he
whined, very upset. "Just to play with!"
"You don't play with food,"
Grandma told him sternly.

Jack's troubles began as soon as he stepped out of the front door. One moment he was walking down the garden path . . .

. . . and the next
he was flying over
the gate . . .

. . . Thud! He landed on the pavement.

"How did I do that?" wondered Jack, amazed. "I didn't mean to jump!" Thinking no more of it, he made his way to school. Then, all of a sudden . . .

Whoosh! He jumped so high he hit his head on a branch.

"I've done it again!" cried Jack as he lay sprawled on the ground. "What on earth is happening to me?"

Then he remembered: the jumping beans!

"Oh no!" he gasped "They're making me jump!"

Very worried, he staggered to his feet. Jack had not gone far when he jumped yet again. This time he found himself sitting on a policeman's shoulders.

"What are you playing at?" demanded
the policeman sternly. "Get off at once!"
"Er, sorry, sir," stammered Jack. "I . . .
It's the jumping beans, you see."
But the policeman only gave him a hard
glare, and Jack quickly hurried off.

Chapter Three

Jack soon came to a busy road. While waiting to cross, he noticed an old lady standing beside him.

"I'll help you cross," offered Jack kindly.

"Oh, thank you," smiled the old lady as Jack took her hand.

No sooner had he done so than both he and the old lady left the ground. Right over the busy traffic they flew and landed on the other side of the road.

"That was a dangerous thing to do!" croaked the old lady, very shaken. "Who do you think you are? Superman?"

Poor Jack had to run all the way to school. Luckily he arrived there without any more troubles.

In class he sat stiffly on his chair, praying he would not jump again.

But he did . . .

Crash! He landed on the teacher's desk.

The class laughed.

But the teacher was not amused.
"Go and stand in the corner!" she
ordered.

Red-faced, Jack obeyed.

In the corner where he stood was a
long pipe running from floor to
ceiling. He held on to it tightly with
both arms. Just in case.

But then he began to jump.
He could not keep his feet
on the floor, no matter
how hard he tried.
Up and
down,
up
and down,
he slid along the pipe.
He looked like a
clockwork toy.
This time even the teacher
had to laugh with the class.

Chapter Four

In the playground things became even
worse for Jack. Now he jumped non-
stop. Boing! Boing! Boing! he went as
if he had springs on his feet.

"Look at Jack! Look at Jack!" cried the children, shrieking and laughing excitedly. "Look at how he's jumping!" A teacher and a dinner lady saw him, and they went to help. They each grabbed Jack by a leg and tried to keep him down.

"Stop jumping!" they shouted.

"I can't help it!" Jack shouted back.

For quite a while all three of them bounced up and down. The other children thought that was hilarious. They laughed all the more.

In the end the teacher and the dinner
lady had to let go of Jack.

"He's completely out of control!" they
panted.

It was true, because Jack was now jumping quicker and higher. He even bounced on the school roof, where the caretaker was doing some repairs.

Jack nearly scared the life out of him.
"I'm going to end up on the moon!"
thought poor Jack worriedly.

Now there was utter chaos in the playground. Everyone tried to get out of Jack's way. They didn't want to be squashed!

"All indoors!" shouted the headmaster. "That boy is getting too dangerous!" And they all rushed inside the school.

The headmaster had had enough.

He decided to call the police. They came at once, with their loud sirens.

But they could not catch Jack. Even with their speedy cars.
"No way!" they said.

Then the school called the fire brigade.
They soon arrived in their bright red
fire engines.

But they could not catch Jack either.

Even with their tall ladders.

"No chance!" they said.

After that the school called the army.
They turned up within minutes, with
their tanks rolling and helicopters
whizzing.

But they could not catch Jack. Even
with their trap nets.
"Impossible!" they said.
They all gave up.

Chapter Five

Then Grandma strode into the
playground, angrily waving her
walking stick.

"Leave my Jack alone!" she ordered.
"He's done nothing wrong. He's just
full of beans!"

"We can see that!" they all replied.

Grandma told them to listen.

She then explained what she had done.

"But I haven't cooked them all," she

added, pulling a handful of beans from

her coat pocket. "See?"

And before anyone could say "Jumping Jack", she swallowed the lot.
"Sorry," she said, grinning, "But it's the only way to catch my Jack."

Chapter Six

The jumping beans worked instantly –
because they were not cooked. All of a
sudden . . . Zoom! Grandma shot up
into the sky like a rocket. She caught
Jack straight away!

Everybody cheered and clapped.

Then, hand in hand, Jack and Grandma bounced out of the school to more cheers and clapping.

"Where're we going?" cried Jack, fed up with jumping.

"Anywhere we like," smiled Grandma. She had wanted to stop Jack jumping, but now she was enjoying herself.

"This is fun!"

They carried on bouncing.

They went over tall buildings . . .

. . . churches, rivers and bridges . . .

. . . parks and football pitches . . .

Then Grandma pulled two large slices
of dark brown cake from her coat
pocket. She handed one to Jack.

"What is it?" asked Jack.

"It's called chocolate concrete," explained Grandma. "I made it very quickly when I heard that you were in trouble. It gets so heavy in your stomach when you eat it, it will stop you jumping. And me!"

Jack gobbled up his chocolate concrete.

"Mmm, not bad at all!" said Grandma, busy munching on her own slice.

"Anyway, it should start working soon."

And it did . . . they started bouncing lower and lower . . . until they stopped completely.

Back home Jack slumped on the sofa. He was exhausted, but also very relieved.

"I will never, ever jump again!" he said. "Never, ever!"

"Oh, you never know," Grandma told him.

"Never, ever!" said Jack again.

But he was wrong. When he was older he became an Olympic champion in the high jump. Jumping Jack won lots of gold medals!

About the Author and Illustrator

A. H. Benjamin is a successful children's author with over twenty books to his name. "I got the idea for 'Jumping Jack' when I learnt that jumping beans really jump," Attia says, "but I would not like to be Jack because I am scared of heights!"

Garry Parsons is an award-winning illustrator of many children's books. He also does artwork for magazines and advertisements. He likes drawing, painting and eating baked beans. "I really like being an illustrator," Garry says, "but I would have loved to have been an Olympic athlete like Jack."

Tips for Beginner Readers

1. Think about the cover and the title of the book. What do you think it will be about? While you are reading, think about what might happen next and why.

2. As you read, ask yourself if what you're reading makes sense. If it doesn't, try rereading or look at the pictures for clues.

3. If there is a word that you do not know, look carefully at the letters, sounds and word parts that you do know. Blend the sounds to read the word. Is this a word you know? Does it make sense in the sentence?

4. Think about the characters, where the story takes place, and the problems the characters in the story faced. What are the important ideas in the beginning, middle and end of the story?

5. Ask yourself questions like:
    Did you like the story?
    Why or why not?
    How did the author make it fun to read?
    How well did you understand it?

Maybe you can understand the story better if you read it again!